Disney
PRINCESS

JOKE
BOOK

For my sister, Jenna,
the funniest girl I know
—C.B.C.

DISNEY PRINCESS

JOKE BOOK

By Courtney Carbone

Illustrated by
Francesco Legramandi, Gabriella Matta,
and the Disney Storybook Art Team

Random House New York

Laughing Matters

The Disney princesses love to laugh with their friends. Telling jokes is a great way to make others smile. By reading and telling the jokes in this book, you can share the magic of happiness with others. Maybe you'll even make up some funny jokes of your own!

Why is Lumiere always smiling?

He's **light**hearted.

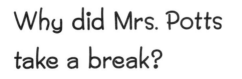

Why did Mrs. Potts take a break?

She was out of **steam**.

What did Chip say when
Belle told him a joke?

"You **crack** me up!"

Which of Belle's friends has four hands but only two arms?

Cogsworth!

What does Cogsworth do when he's hungry?

He goes back **four seconds**!

What did the plates tell Belle on
her first night in the castle?

"Dinner is on us!"

What is champagne's
favorite type of music?

Pop!

How does Lumiere impress his guests?

He treats them to a **light** meal!

What did everyone think of the
party decorations?

They were just the icing on the cake.

Why did Belle twirl
around the castle?

She wanted to take her
new dress for a **spin**.

What kind of robe can't be worn?

A ward**robe**!

What did the townspeople call Belle's dinner party?

Beauty and the **feast**!

What does the Beast eat for breakfast?

Whatever he wants!

Why is the library the biggest
room in the Beast's castle?

It has the most **stories**!

What happened when the Beast
bumped into a bookshelf?

He **nudged** a book by its cover!

What is Gaston's favorite drink?

Punch!

Why did the girl trip on her dress?

She was head over heels for Gaston!

Why is Cogsworth good
at telling jokes?

Timing is everything!

Why is it easy to
wake up Lumiere?

He's a **light** sleeper!

Why did Merida tie a ribbon around her arrows?

She needed a **bow**!

Did you hear about the Highland Games?

They were **in tents**!

What did Merida give her brothers?

Bear hugs!

Why did Merida have the triplets put on socks?

They had **bear** feet!

What is Elinor's favorite ice cream?

Cookies and **Queen**.

Was it hard for Merida to trick her mother?

No, it was a piece of **cake**!

Why does Merida ride her horse, Angus?

Because he's too heavy to carry!

Where is Angus's favorite place to go for a ride?

Around the **neigh**borhood.

What happened when Merida tried to catch the blue lights in the fog?

She **mist**!

What did Tiana's parents sing
to her when she was a baby?

A lulla**bayou**.

Have you heard
the story of the
princess and the
frog?

It's **ribbit**-ing!

What happened to Tiana
and Naveen?

They lived **hoppily** ever after!

Why did Tiana run to the store?

She was out of **thyme!**

How did Tiana fix the smashed tomato?

She used tomato **paste!**

How does Tiana like her herbs?
In **mint** condition.

Why did Naveen feel like he was being watched?

Because potatoes have **eyes**!

Why doesn't Tiana tell secrets in her kitchen?

Because the corn has **ears**!

Why did Tiana give Naveen a job at her restaurant?

He **kneaded** dough!

What is Naveen's favorite game?

Leapfrog!

Why is Flit a hummingbird?

Because he doesn't know the words!

When does Pocahontas not use her ears?

When she listens with her heart!

Why did Grandma Willow
say goodbye?

It was time to **leaf**.

What did Grandma Willow
take on vacation?

Her **trunk**!

What is Pocahontas's
favorite type of ship?

Friend**ship**.

Why is Captain John Smith
such a good sailor?

Because he knows
the **ropes**!

Can Pocahontas paddle a boat
by herself?

Of course! **Canoe?**

Why do Meiko, Flit, and Pocahontas
get along so well?

They are all in the
same **boat**!

Where does Pocahontas keep
her money?
In the river**bank**!

What is Meiko's favorite dance?

The **polka**hontas.

Why does Pocahontas run through the cornfields?

They are a-**maize**-ing!

Why are Cinderella's bird
friends so helpful?

They always
flock together!

What do birds
dream about?

Living happily
feather after!

What is Gus's favorite game?

Hide-and-**squeak**.

What does Jaq like to eat
for dessert?

Mice cream!

Why were Anastasia and Drizella sitting on the stairs?

They are Cinderella's **step**sisters!

What does Cinderella's stepmother think of her cat, Lucifer?

She thinks he's **purr**-fect!

Why did Lucifer and Bruno go outside?

They heard it was raining cats and dogs!

What happened when Lucifer got stuck in the rain?

It was a cat-astrophe!

Why did Bruno chase his tail?

He wanted to make ends meet!

Why was Cinderella so happy?

She was having a **ball**!

What did the mice want for Cinderella?

A fairy-**tail** ending.

What did Cinderella say about the dress the mice made?

"It's **sew** beautiful!"

How did the Prince
know Cinderella
was the one?

She is his
sole mate!

Why is Prince Charming excited
for his coronation?

It will be a **crowning** achievement.

Why is it so dark inside Cinderella
and Prince Charming's castle?

It is full of **knights**!

Knock, Knock.
Who's there?

Bibbidi bobbidi.
Bibbidi bobbidi who?

You must be Cinderella's
fairy godmother!

What is the
Fairy Godmother's
favorite color?

Bibbidi bobbidi **blue**

How did the Fairy Godmother
fix her broken wand?

Bibbidi bobbidi glue!

What advice would the
Fairy Godmother give
to a cow?

Bibbidi bobbidi moo!

Who sings outside Snow White's window in winter?

Brrrds!

Why is Snow White so precious to the Dwarfs?

She has a heart of gold!

What is the Dwarfs' favorite snack?

Cottage cheese!

Why is Snow White a good problem solver?

Because she's the **fairest** of them all.

What do the Seven Dwarfs say
when they get to the cottage?

"We're **heigh-home!**"

Why don't the Dwarfs want
to get new jobs?

They have a **mine**
of their own!

How do Ariel's friends call
each other?

On their **shell** phones.

Why did Eric want to buy
a new boat?

There was a big **sail**!

Why do sailors make good husbands?

They know how to tie the **knot**!

Where does Flounder sleep?

On a **water**bed!

Why does Scuttle the seagull
live by the sea?

Because if he lived by the bay,
he would be a **bay**gull!

Why did Scuttle think the ocean
was saying hello?

It **waved**!

Why is Ariel so good at singing?

She knows a range of **scales**!

What is Ariel's favorite dessert?

Saltwater taffy.

What did Flounder say
to Sebastian?

"**Water** you up to?"

How did Sebastian
know he was getting
a surprise party?

He smelled
something fishy!

What did Sebastian yell when
he got tangled in seaweed?

"**Kelp!**"

Why do Ariel's sisters like to sing bass notes?

They stay out of **treble**!

What do mermaids learn in school?

The A-B-**Seas**!

What game did the mermaids play after voice lessons?

Musical chairs!

Why are Ariel's fish friends so smart?

Because they live in **schools**!

What kind of horse doesn't walk, trot, or gallop?

A sea horse!

What is an oyster's favorite color?

Pearl-ple.

Why did Flotsam and
Jetsam cross the ocean?

To get to the other **tide**.

What did Flounder get
from an angry shark?

As far away as possible!

Why does King Triton live in salt water?

Because **pepper** makes him sneeze!

Who are the strongest creatures in Atlantica?

The **mussels!**

What did Rapunzel tell Pascal?

"Don't ever **change**!"

What is Pascal's biggest worry?

That he won't **blend** in.

Why doesn't Pascal like to dance?

He has two left feet!

What do you get when you mix Pascal and Maximus?

A horse of a different color!

Why did Maximus chew with his mouth open?

He had bad **stable** manners!

What is a bunny's favorite game?

Hopscotch!

What kind of jewelry does a rabbit wear?

24-**carrot** gold!

What did Rapunzel say when
she arrived in town?

"**Hair** I am!"

What is Aurora's favorite color?

Forest green!

What did Prince Philip call Aurora when she was cleaning?

Sweeping Beauty.

What is Aurora's favorite letter of the alphabet?

Zzzz.

What kind of flower
is hidden in the forest?

The Briar **Rose**.

How do the three good fairies
get around?

They **wing** it!

Why doesn't Sleeping Beauty
use an umbrella?

She always has Merry**weather**!

What did Flora say to Fauna?

"Have a **wand**-erful day!"

What is Jasmine's favorite jewel?

A **diamond** in the rough.

What is Aladdin's favorite kind of rice?

Jasmine!

Why wasn't Abu in the town parade?

He was too busy **monkey**ing around.

What did the Genie give
to the sea captain?

Three **fishes**!

Why isn't the Genie afraid of the dark?

He always has a lamp!

Why is Rajah so good at hide-and-seek?

Because he's never **spotted**!

What did Jasmine ask Rajah?

"**Orange** you glad we're friends?"

What does Cri-Kee use to eat dinner?

Hopsticks!

Why couldn't Mushu keep up with Mulan?

He was **dragon** his feet!

Why did Mulan ride Khan into battle?

She needed to **hoof** it!

Why did Shang believe Mulan was a man?

She had a good **Ping** going.

Why is Mulan a good artist?

She knows how to **draw** a sword.

Why didn't Mulan use the pencil?

It was **point**less!

What did Mulan say when she gave
Little Brother a treat?

"**Bone** appétit!"

What did Mulan tell Little Brother?

"We'll be friends **fur**ever!"